Bibble and the Bubbles

Maverick
Early Readers

'Bibble and the Bubbles'
An original concept by Alice Hemming

Illustrated by Sara Sanchez

Published by MAVERICK ARTS PUBLISHING LTD

Studio 3A, City Business Centre, 6 Brighton Road,

Horsham, West Sussex, RH13 5BB

+44 (0)1403 256941

A CIP catalogue record for this book is available at the British Library.

ISBN 978-1-84886-224-1

Maverick
arts publishing
www.maverickbooks.co.uk

Blue

This book is rated as: Blue Band (Guided Reading)
The original picture book text for this story has been modified by the author to be an early reader.

Bibble and the Bubbles

by Alice Hemming
illustrated by Sara Sanchez

Bobby blew lots of bubbles.

Some of the bubbles popped.

Some of the bubbles floated

up, up, up into the sky.

Where did they go?

Bibble lived in space,

millions of miles away.

Bibble liked catching bubbles.

One day, the bubbles stopped.

Bibble wanted to find out why.

Bibble built a bubble spaceship!

He went to find the bubbles.

Bibble landed in Bobby's garden.

"What's your name?" asked Bobby.

“Bibble” said Bibble.

“My name is Bobby” said Bobby.

Bibble made a little bubble spaceship for Bobby.

It was just like the one

he came to Earth in.

When there was no bubble mix left

Bobby and Bibble made some more.

Bobby and Bibble blew lots of bubbles.

Bibble made bubble animals...

and even rode a bubble bicycle!

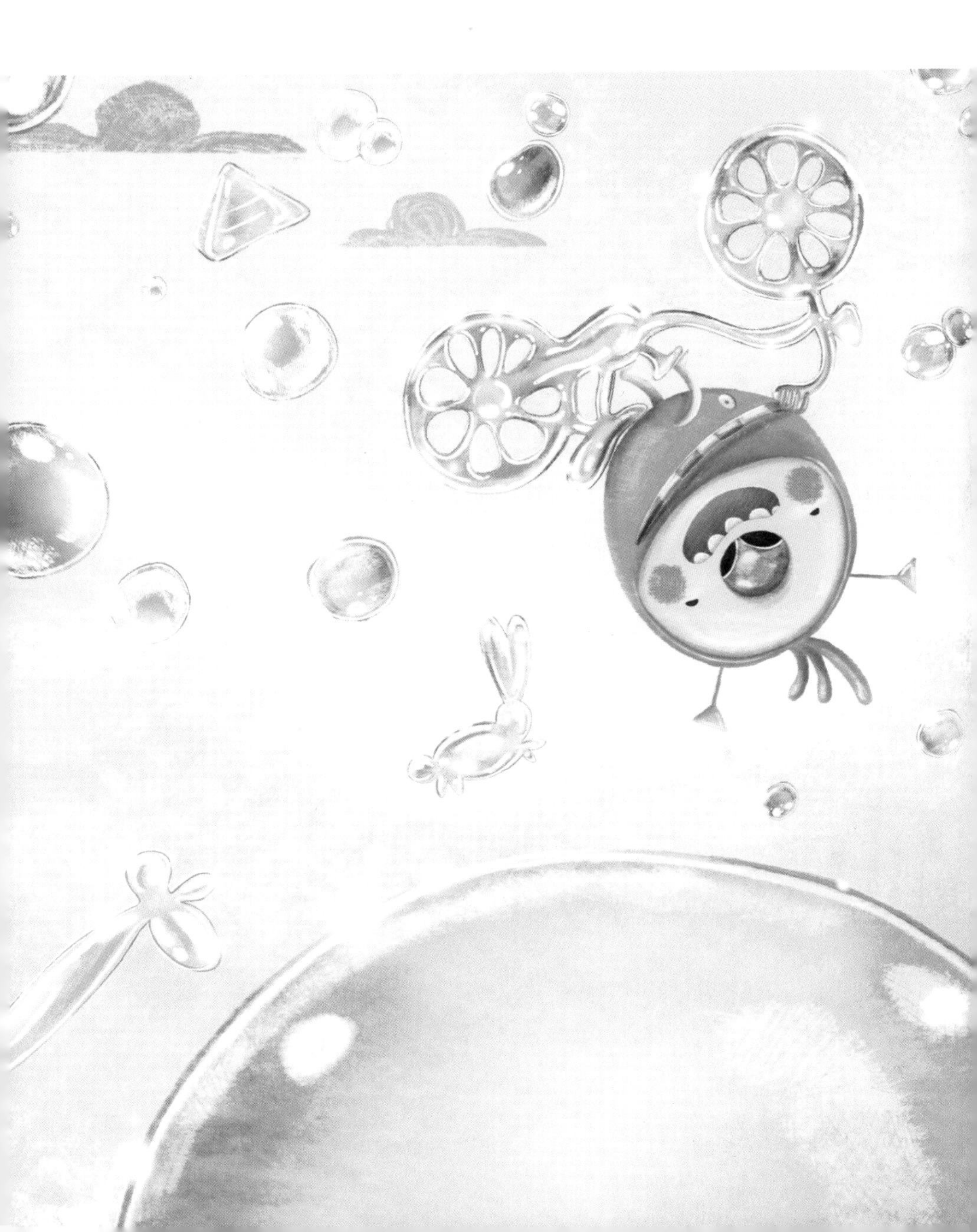

Bobby and Bibble had lots of fun.

Then Bibble had to go home.

Bobby waved goodbye.

He felt sad.

But Bibble left a special gift:

a bubble that didn't pop.

Now Bobby feels happy.

Maybe Bibble will come back one day.

Quiz

1. Where does Bibble live?
a) In space
b) In a shed
c) In a forest

2. What does Bibble build?
a) A bubble house
b) A bubble car
c) A bubble spaceship

3. Why does Bibble leave Bobby?
a) He goes to visit a friend
b) He wants to find more bubbles
c) He has to go home

4. What present does Bibble leave for Bobby?

a) A bubble bicycle

b) A bubble that does not pop

c) A bubble hat

5. Why does Bibble visit Bobby?

a) He wants to know where bubbles come from

b) He wants to make new friends

c) He wants to make some bubble mixture

Turn over for answers

Book Bands for Guided Reading

The Institute of Education book banding system is a scale of colours that reflects the various levels of reading difficulty. The bands are assigned by taking into account the content, the language style, the layout and phonics.

Maverick Early Readers are a bright, attractive range of books covering the pink to purple bands. All of these books have been book banded for guided reading to the industry standard and edited by a leading educational consultant.

For more titles visit:
www.maverickbooks.co.uk/early-readers

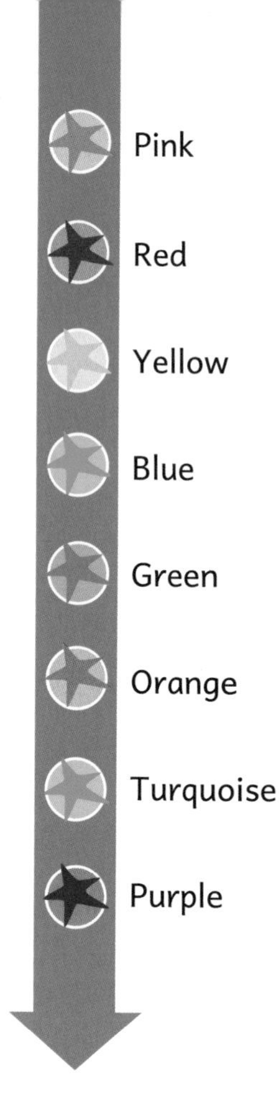

Fast Fox and Slow Snail 978-1-84886-295-1
Mine, Mine, Mine Said the Porcupine 978-1-84886-296-8
The Smart Hat 978-1-84886-294-4
Strictly No Crocs 978-1-84886-240-1
Bibble and the Bubbles 978-1-84886-224-1

Quiz Answers: 1a, 2c, 3c, 4b, 5a